Liliana's Grandmothers

To Cristina, Camilo, and Luis

Distributed in Canada by Douglas & McIntyre Ltd.
Color separations by Hong Kong Scanner Arts
Printed and bound in the United States of America by Berryville Graphics
Typography by Caitlin Martin
First edition, 1998

Library of Congress Cataloging-in-Publication Data
Torres, Leyla.
Liliana's grandmothers / Leyla Torres. — 1st ed.
p. cm.
Summary: Because one of her grandmothers lives down the street and the other in a faraway country, Liliana experiences two very different ways of life when she visits them.
ISBN 0-374-35105-8
[1. Grandmothers—Fiction.] I. Title.
PZ7.T6457Li 1998
[E]—dc21 97-37256

Liliana's Grandmothers

LEYLA TORRES

Farrar Straus Giroux New York

Liliana's grandmothers are Mima and Mama Gabina.

Mima lives on the same street as Liliana in a town where summer days are long and winter brings lots of snow. Sometimes Liliana visits Mima for the afternoon. Other times, her parents let her spend the night.

Mama Gabina lives in another country, so Liliana has to travel by plane to see her. Liliana's parents send her to visit for a week or two at a time. Mama Gabina speaks only Spanish, and in the city where she lives the weather is warm all year round.

When Liliana stays overnight at Mima's, they do yoga exercises early in the morning. Mima has a cat named Suzzy, who watches them. Suzzy sticks out her tongue, even when she is sleeping.

Mama Gabina feeds and sings to her birds first thing in the morning. Liliana's favorite is a parrot named Roberto, who always says, *"Buenos días. ¿Quiere cacao?"*—"Good morning. Do you want cocoa?"

Mima makes quilts to raise funds for her church. Liliana helps sew the squares and triangles of fabric together.

Mama Gabina has a garden where she grows flowers and vegetables. She says that talking to the plants makes them grow healthy and strong. Liliana greets each plant: *"Hola, preciosa, ¡qué bien luces hoy!"*— "Hi, precious. You look great today!"

Mima serves a small lunch. A peanut butter and jelly sandwich with a glass of apple juice is enough. But dinner is a feast!

Mama Gabina prepares a big lunch. Liliana's favorite is kidney beans in tomato sauce, avocado salad, and rice. Dinner is often small—a tamale, a slice of papaya, and a glass of milk.

SUBWAY
Leyla Torres
LIFE

When Liliana stops by to see Mima after school, Mima reads stories to her. Mima's voice is so soft and soothing that Liliana has a hard time staying awake.

Mama Gabina takes a siesta in the afternoon. Liliana likes to nap, too, but it's often hard to sleep because Mama Gabina snores so loud.

Sometimes Liliana is mischievous and has fun startling her grandmothers. She knows that Mima is afraid of mice . . .

. . . and that Mama Gabina is afraid of frogs!

Mima likes to do crossword puzzles. Liliana and Mima spend time together trying to find the right words.

Mama Gabina dances the Cumbia.
Liliana dreams of someday being
as good a dancer as she is.

After dinner, Mima sits by the window and tells Liliana stories about her childhood. Liliana especially enjoys the ones about Marcelle, the grumpy French lady who cooked for Mima's grandparents.

Mama Gabina also tells stories at the end of the day. Liliana likes to hear Mama Gabina talk about how she met her husband, Liliana's grandfather, at the festival of San Pascual.

Many nights, after her parents have tucked her into bed, Liliana closes her eyes and remembers the laughter and joy of Mima and Mama Gabina. Whether down the street or in another country, Liliana's grandmothers are never far away in her thoughts.